KEESHIG & THE OJIBWE PTERODACTYLS

Story by
Keeshig Spade as told to Celeste Pedri-Spade

Illustrations by
Robert Spade and Kiniw Spade

October 2019

Published by Kegedonce Press
11 Park Road
Neyaashiinigmiing, ON N0H 2T0
www.kegedonce.com
Administration Office/Book Orders
P.O. Box 517
Owen Sound, ON N4K 5R1

Printed in Canada by Ball Media
Cover Illustration: Robert Spade
Illustrations: Robert Spade and Kiniw Spade
Design: Chantal Lalonde Design

Library and Archives Canada Cataloguing in Publication

Title: Keeshig & the Ojibwe pterodactyls / story by Keeshig Spade ; as told to Celeste Pedri-Spade
 ; illustrations by Robert Spade and Kiniw Spade.
Other titles: Keeshig and the Ojibwe pterodactyls
Names: Spade, Keeshig, 2012- author. | Pedri-Spade, Celeste, 1982- author. | Spade, Robert, 1975-
 illustrator. | Spade, Kiniw, 2013- illustrator.
Identifiers: Canadiana 20190127635 | ISBN 9781928120209 (softcover)
Classification: LCC PS8637.P3 K44 2019 | DDC jC813/.6—dc23

For Customer Service/Orders
Tel 1–800–591–6250 Fax 1–800–591–6251
100 Armstrong Ave. Georgetown, ON L7G 5S4
Email orders@litdistco.ca or visit www.kegedonce.com
We acknowledge the support of the Canada Council for the Arts which last year invested $20.1 million in
writing and publishing throughout Canada.

We would like to acknowledge funding support from the Ontario Arts Council, an agency of the
Government of Ontario.

This book belongs to:

For two great teachers:
Uncle Joseph & Uncle Art

One hot summer day after a powwow, Keeshig and his family go to the beach for a swim. They are hot after dancing all day and need to cool off. While his younger brothers and dad are busy getting changed out of their regalia, Keeshig and his mom walk ahead to the water's edge to feel the cool breeze off the lake.

As Keeshig and his mom stand on the shore of Gitchee Gumee (sometimes called Lake Superior) they see Nanaboozhoo in the distance.

3

Nanaboozhoo reveals himself as a big piece of land. He looks like a giant man lying on his back, taking a nap in the great big lake. People have different names for Nanaboozhoo depending on who they are and where they come from. Some people call him Weaskejak or Glooscap, while others call him the Sleeping Giant.

"Mom, I can see Nanaboozhoo!"

Keeshig is excited to see Nanaboozhoo for he is a great teacher that teaches people many things about life.

Nanaboozhoo knows about things like animals, plants, and humans. For example Nanaboozhoo helps teach us the importance of being patient and being helpful to others.

 "All the Ojibwe pterodactyls live over there with Nanaboozhoo!" Keeshig says.

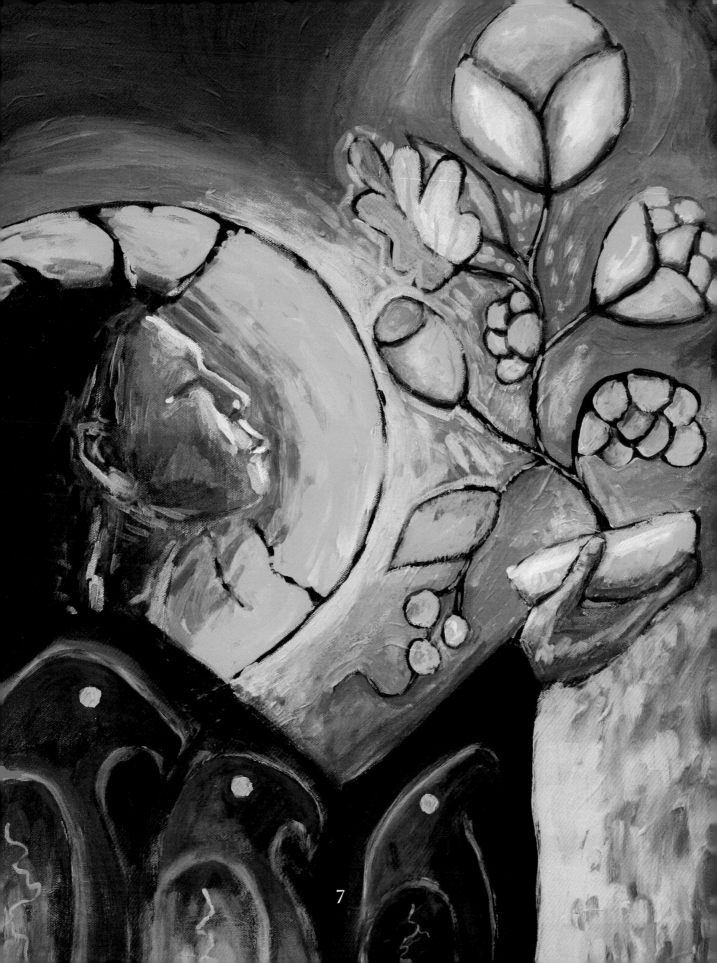

Keeshig's mom is confused.
"Ojibwe pterodactyls?" she asks.

"Yes, you know...the Thunderbirds!"
Keeshig replies.

Keeshig's mom smiles and asks,
"I wonder what they are doing
right now?"

"Well, it is afternoon, so they are out hunting," answers Keeshig.

"What do you think they like to eat?" Keeshig's mom asks. "Maybe mooz (moose)? Or hamburger soup?"

"No way, Mom," Keeshig says. "They like to eat big fish!"

"Fish?" asks Keeshig's mom. "What kind of fish…ogaa (pickerel?)"

"Nope. They eat ginoozhe (northern pike)," says Keeshig, "…and big puffy snakes. Nanaboozhoo looks after the Ojibwe pterodactyls when they are hunting."

"I see," replies Keeshig's mom. "Just like your dad and I look after you and your brothers."

"Look, Mom!" Keeshig blurts out. "Nanaboozhoo is with the Ojibwe pterodactyls right now!" He looks at his mom. "They are Nanaboozhoo's heart, you know."

"Do you mean, they hunt near his heart?" Keeshig's mom asks while gazing at the napping Nanaboozhoo.

"No, Mom. They are his heart!"
Keeshig explains. "When we hear
the thunder coming from the sky
and it gets really, really, loud, it is the
Thunderbird beating its wings in
Nanaboozhoo's chest!"

Keeshig's mom gives him a big
hug. "Just as the Thunderbirds are
Nanaboozhoo's heart, you and your
brothers are my heart Keeshig!
Your stories make me feel so happy
and thankful. They are such good
medicine."

Keeshig Spade (Keeshigbahnahnkut) is a seven year-old Anishinabe from Lac des Mille Lacs First Nation. He currently resides with his family in Sudbury, ON where he attends Alexander Public School. Keeshig enjoys being a big brother to Kiniw and Wakinyan and he enjoys doing many things with them including playing outside, swimming and dancing men's traditional at powwows. Keeshig is a member of the Sturgeon Clan and has a gift for sharing stories and singing songs. Keeshig's favorite time of the year is when he gets to go back west in the summer to be with his kookums and great kookum.

Dr. Celeste Pedri-Spade (Anang Onimiwin) is an Anishinabekwe from Lac des Mille Lacs First Nation. She is a mother, wife, researcher, learner and artist. Celeste is an Assistant Professor in the School of Northern and Community Studies at Laurentian University where she also teaches in the School of Indigenous Relations. She is also the inaugural Director of the Maamwizing Indigenous Research Institute.

Robert Spade (Keeshigooninii) is an Anishinabe artist-educator from Northern Ontario (Fort Hope First Nation). Rob is a father, husband, artist, sundancer, teacher (Sturgeon Clan), and has many years of experience delivering cultural and arts-based education, counseling and support, cultural sensitivity training, cultural-arts-based therapy and guidance to Indigenous and non-Indigenous children, youth, and adults. Rob has spent over half his life living and working out on the land in his traditional territory learning teachings and stories, ceremonies, traditional skills and art from his Elders. He is a gifted and accomplished storyteller, men's traditional dancer, drummer, singer, and visual artist.

Kiniw Spade (Nitaw Gamik) is a six year-old Anishinabe from Lac des Mille Lacs First Nation. He currently resides with his family in Sudbury, ON and attends Alexander Public School. Kiniw enjoys spending time with his brothers, Keeshig and Wakinyan, and the rest of his family. He loves spending his time visiting, playing with small animal toys, dancing men's traditional, reading books and painting. His favourite birds are the woodpecker and seagull.